Sunne is a magical being or "magbee." Nyame, the Creator of the planet Wiase, imbues Sunne with the power of the sun. Sunne's straight-haired siblings, Earthe, Watre, and Winde, have unique powers of their own.

When Sunne is teased and bullied by siblings because of Sunne's kinky and spirally afro-textured hair, Sunne desperately tries to change. Join Sunne and the other magbees, as they learn that there is beauty and power in difference. The message of self-love and bullying prevention in Sunne's Gift, coupled with its sci-fi imagery, make it a hit with people of all ages.

About the Author

Ama Karikari-Yawson,Esq. earned her BA from Harvard University, an MBA from the Wharton School, and a JD from the University of Pennsylvania Law School. Her unique understanding of social issues, business, and the law has enabled her to become a relevant voice and sought-after speaker on issues as varied as education, cultural sensitivity, bullying, sexual violence, and personal empowerment.

In 2013, a painful experience with bullying inspired her to write her best-selling fable about difference, *Sunne's Gift*. Ms. Karikari-Yawson became so personally invested in spreading the book's message of healing and harmony that she quit her six-figure job as a securities lawyer to become a full-time, author, storyteller, and educator.

Through her company, Milestales Publishing and Education Consulting, she publishes and distributes books and lesson plans. Additionally, she facilitates life-changing workshops and training sessions that incorporate storytelling, drama, dance, history, cutting edge psychological research, and legal analysis in order to truly propel participants towards healthier and more successful lives.

Her other books include the *Kwanzaa Nana Is Coming to Town* series, which introduces a folkloric character to the Kwanzaa holiday. She can be reached at milestalespublishing.gmail.com, and you can follow her work at https://www.facebook.com/milestales and www.milestales.com.

About the Illustrator

Rashad is a graduate of Tufts University, graduating with a BA in

Anthropology and a minor in Mandarin Chinese Language and Culture. His interests and passions are varied, ranging from the study of people and culture to performance art, fine art, and fiction writing.

He is also a self-taught freelance illustrator and aspiring animator, specializing in fantasy/sci-fi and cartoon illustration, using digital, pencil and pen mediums.

Mr. Malik Davis thoroughly enjoyed working on *Sunne's Gift* and is deeply committed to sharing its message of self-love, self-acceptance, and bullying prevention.

Please like Rashad's work on Facebook:
https://www.facebook.com/ramalikillustrations.

SUNNE'S GIFT

Sunne's Gift
By Ama Karikari Yawson
First Edition (Softcover)

Graphic Design by Daisy Lew and Emil Rivera
Illustration by Rashad Malik Davis

The intent of the author and publisher is to inspire each reader to love and respect his or her own God-given gifts and those of others. Although the author and publisher cannot assume responsibility for the awesome feats that each reader will achieve with this renewed love and respect, they wish that they could.

Published by Milestales: Stories That Help Us Go The Distance
www.milestales.com

ISBN 978-0-9914808-3-8

Please enjoy these other Milestales titles!
Sunne's Gift: How Sunne Overcame Bullying to Reclaim God's Gift (Hardcover)
Sunne's Gift Spanish and English Activity Book: Libro de Actividades El Don de Sunne

We're Making The World A Better Place:
Uplifting Stories and Creative Activities for Young People (Kwanzaa Nana Series)

_____ loves you

and purchased this spectacular book for you, _____,

because like Sunne, you are different. You are like no other person in the universe.

This book will help you to always remember that your unique qualities make you

both BEAUTIFUL and POWERFUL. Continue to revel in your own truth.

In the beginning, the planet Wiase was not as it is today.

There was no sun to provide warmth or light.
There was no earth from which fruit,
vegetables, or flowers could grow.
There was no water to quench the thirst of the living.
There was no wind to transport seeds or
provide a refreshing breeze.

The Creator, Nyame, had become bored with the barren planet Wiase. In an instant, and with just a thought, Nyame brought forth the sun, earth, water, and wind. Sunshine illuminated lush vegetation growing from the brilliant earth. The sounds of water flowing and breezes blowing produced a beautiful melody.

It was so good. But Nyame wanted to create more planets. "I'll make children to help me take care of this planet, Wiase." Nyame said. In an instant, and with just a thought, Nyame brought forth four magical beings or "magbees": Sunne, Earthe, Watre, and Winde.

Nyame addressed the magbees.

"Sunne, you are imbued with the power of the sun. For this reason, your skin is sun-darkened red, and your hair grows in spirally twists toward the sun. Take care of yourself, for the sun dwells within you."

"Earthe, you are imbued with the power of the earth. For this reason,
your skin is brown, and your straight hair grows toward the soil.
Take care of yourself, for the earth dwells within you."

"Watre, you are imbued with the power of water. For this reason, your skin is translucent green, and your straight hair flows down your back like water. Take care of yourself, for the waters dwell within you."

"Last, Winde, you are imbued with the power of the wind.
For this reason, your skin is gray, and your straight hair blows
with the breeze. Take care of yourself, for the wind dwells within you."

"You are all my children, made
in my image. Love one another
and treasure each other's gifts.
Goodbye and I love you all."
Nyame's voice faded, as Nyame
went off to create other planets.

The four magbees were
very responsible.

Sunne did a wave
dance every morning
and evening to make
the sun rise and set.

By doing hip circles
every afternoon,
Earthe put nutrients
into the soil.

When the soil became dry,
Watre did finger jiggles to
summon the rain.

Winde blew out gaseous gusts of air that carried seeds to new places.

14

In their spare time, the magbees climbed trees
and played hide-and-seek. They also sang.
"Prim pra na na, prim pra na na, we are having so much fun!
Prim pra na na, prim pra na na, taking care of Wiase for everyone."

One day, the four magbees travelled to a river. They looked down at their reflections. For the first time, it occurred to them that Sunne looked different. Earthe, Winde, and Watre all had hair that lay flat and grew downward. But Sunne's hair stood tall.

Earthe was confused about the difference and asked,
"Why did Nyame give Sunne different hair?"
Winde wanted special hair, too. Jealously, Winde blurted,
"Sunne, your hair is ugly. Your spirals look totally ridiculous!"
Watre thought that Sunne's hair was beautiful
but did not want to feel left out so Watre said,
"Yeah, your hair is really weird!"

18

Sunne's heart sank. Tears formed in Sunne's eyes.
Sunne did not want to be different, ugly, ridiculous, or weird.

Sunne picked up a stick and began to beat each spiral
of hair to make it straight. With each slap, Sunne's head
ached and Sunne felt weaker. But Sunne continued,
as Earthe, Winde, and Watre began to sing.

"You must! You must! It's worth the fuss!
Soon you will look like the rest of us!"

But when the last
spiral of hair became
straight, all of Sunne's
hair fell out.

The sun disappeared,
and darkness descended
upon the land. Sunne, Earthe,
Winde, and Watre looked
around in horror!

Sunne did the wave dance again and again, but still there was no sun. Earthe, Watre, and Winde tried to do the wave dance, but still there was no sun. In a flash, the words of Nyame came to them.

"Sunne, you are imbued with the power of the sun. For this reason, your skin is sun-darkened red, and your hair grows in spirally twists toward the sun. Take care of yourself, for the sun dwells within you." By destroying Sunne's gift of spirally hair, they had destroyed Sunne's power of the sun.

The silver glow of the moon did
not provide enough light for their
games. The fruit trees, corn, and other
vegetation began to die. The magbees
felt weak with hunger.

In their collective grief, they chanted
"Nyame! Nyame! We are so sorry for what we have done.
We have destroyed our power of the sun!
Oh how, oh how can our mistake be undone?"
They waited for Nyame to answer. They could feel Nyame's presence,
but they did not hear Nyame's voice. The magbees sat and cried.

Finally Nyame said, "My children,
I forgive you all. I see that you have
learned your lesson. I made no mistakes
in creating you all with your beautiful and
varied colors, hair types, and features. You
all are equal in power but distinct in your
gifts. Never destroy your own gift because
you covet someone else's. I love you all."
Nyame's voice faded.

At that moment, Sunne's spirally twists
grew back, and the sun reappeared. Sunne
felt alive and powerful again.
The magbees jumped up and down with
glee, thanking Nyame.

Then, the magbees
walked back to the
river and looked at
themselves again.

31

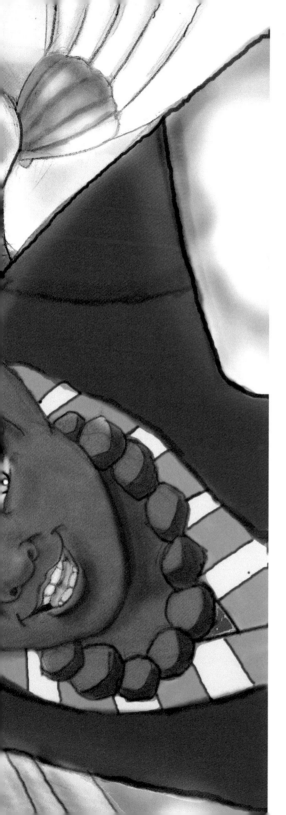

Sunne admired the beauty reflected. Sunne said, "I should not have destroyed my hair. My lovely spirals are what make me special and what makes me special makes me great. Earthe, Watre, and Winde agreed, and then all of the children sang.

"Sunne's beautiful: we can't deny!
In Sunne's hair, the sun's power lies.
We're all special in our own way.
We should celebrate each other
every day!"

SELF-ESTEEM BUILDING QUESTIONS

PSYCHO-SOCIAL STUDIES

1 • In the story, Nyame created the planet Wiase and the magbees with thoughts. What do you create with your thoughts?

2 • In the story, Nyame made the magbees different because they represented different forces of nature. Why do you think that human beings have different colors and features?

3 • In the story, Earthe, Watre, and Winde bullied Sunne by saying Sunne's hair is different, ugly, ridiculous, and weird. Go back to the text of the story. What were the three emotions or mental states that motivated Earthe, Watre, and Winde to be mean to Sunne?

4 • How should have Earthe, Watre, and Winde managed those three emotions or mental states? What should they have said to Sunne?

5 • Unfortunately, Earthe, Watre, and Winde did engage in bullying in the story. How do you think that Sunne should have reacted to Earthe, Watre, and Winde's bullying behavior?

6 • Have you ever been teased or teased other people? Please describe your own experience.

7 • Do you ever feel like changing yourself to fit in? Please describe your own experience.

8 • Sunne's special gift was the sun. What special gifts do you have?

9 • What would happen to the world if you did not share your gift?

10 • How will you continue to nurture your gifts and talents for the benefit of the world?

Dear parents, teachers, and children, Can you please share your answers with us by going to https://www.facebook.com/milestales/ ?

SUNNE'S PLEDGE

I am a magbee, a magical being.
The Creator made no mistakes when creating me.
Every hair on my head is beautiful.
Every inch of my skin is divine.
My face, body, mind and spirit are all unique reflections of God's handiwork.
My intellectual powers are infinite.
My creative gifts know no bounds.
I promise to honor and nurture all of my gifts.
I will disregard any negative comments, ridicule, teasing or bullying
directed at me.
I know my power, value and worth.
In short, I will be free to be me.
I promise to encourage others to do the same.

*Signature:*_____   *Date:*_____

37985043R00024